THE GINGERBREAD COWBOY

By Janet Squires

Illustrated by Holly Berry

LAURA GERINGER BOOKS

An Imprint of HarperCollins Publishers

The Gingerbread Cowboy
Text copyright © 2006 by Janet Squires
Illustrations copyright © 2006 by Holly Berry
Manufactured in China.

For information address HarperCollins Children's Books, a division of HarperCollins
Publishers, 1350 Avenue of the Americas, New York, NY 10019.
www.harperchildrens.com

Library of Congress Cataloging-in-Publication Data
Squires, Janet.
    The Gingerbread Cowboy / by Janet Squires ; illustrated by Holly Berry.—1st ed.
        p.   cm.
    "Laura Geringer Books."
    Summary: A freshly baked gingerbread cowboy escapes from the ranch kitchen
and eludes his pursuers in this western United States version of the Gingerbread boy.
    ISBN-10: 0-06-077863-6 – ISBN-10: 0-06-077864-4 (lib. bdg.)
    ISBN-13: 978-0-06-077863-7 – ISBN-13: 978-0-06-077864-4 (lib. bdg.)
    [1. Folklore.   2. Fairy tales.]   I. Berry, Holly, ill.   II. Gingerbread boy. English.
III. Title.
PZ8.S4674 Gin 2006   2005013915
[398.21 21]–dc21   CIP
                                                                                         AC

Typography by Alicia Mikles
7 8 9 10
❖
First Edition

To Katherine, with love.
Your enthusiasm is contagious.
—J.S.

To Tyler—the brand-new cowboy
—H.B.

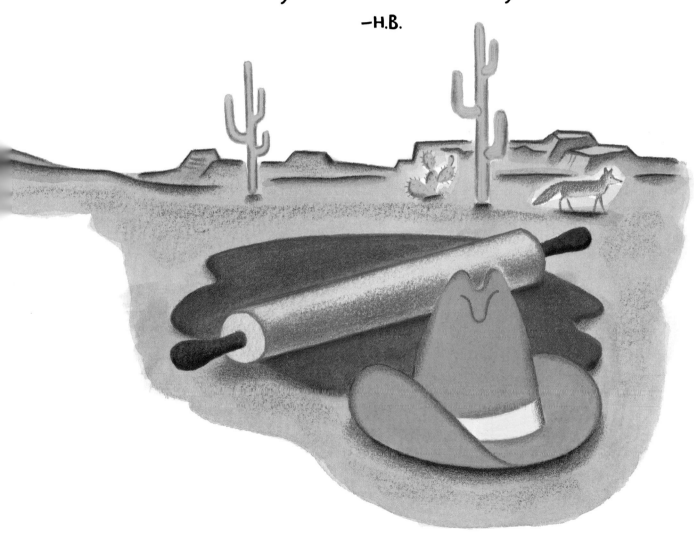

ONCE UPON A TIME

in the Wild Wild West, there lived a rancher and his wife. Every morning, just as the sun was coming up, the rancher saddled his horses and fed the cattle while his wife baked biscuits. Biscuits with butter, biscuits with honey, biscuits with jelly . . . Yes, those breakfast biscuits were plump as pillows, soft as clouds, and tasty as a big Texas barbecue.

Then one day, just as the sun was coming up, the rancher's wife decided she was tired of making biscuits.

So she measured and mixed, and she made gingerbread dough.

She rolled that dough flat and cut out the shape of a boy—but not just any boy. He had boots on his feet. He had a hat on his head. And he had a big belt buckle made of spun sugar.

He was a Gingerbread Cowboy!

She took raisins, candies, and nuts and gave him two bright eyes, a laughing mouth, and a cowboy vest with fringe. And she put him in the oven to bake.

SUN RISE

VANILLA

5 oz.

"I sure am hungry for biscuits," said the rancher, leaning over and sniffing the rodeo-romping good smell coming out of the oven. He opened the door for a peek.

And as quick as the flick of a cow pony's tail, out jumped the Gingerbread Cowboy! And he ran out the door as fast as his boots could carry him.

"Whoa!" shouted the rancher.

"Come back!" cried his wife.

But the Gingerbread Cowboy just laughed and said, "Giddyup, giddyup as fast as you can. You can't catch me, I'm the Gingerbread Man."

He jumped over a horned lizard gobbling up ants and
raced away as fast as his boots could carry him . . .

until he came to a roadrunner. "I was about to have lizard for breakfast," said the roadrunner. "But I think I'll eat you instead."

The Gingerbread Cowboy just laughed and said, "Giddyup, giddyup as fast as you can. You can't catch me, I'm the Gingerbread Man." He wriggled through the corral fence and raced away as fast as his boots could carry him . . .

until he came to a band of javelinas munching on cactus pads. "Gingerbread!" shouted the javelinas. "Yee-haw!"

The Gingerbread Cowboy just laughed and said, "Giddyup, giddyup as fast as you can. You can't catch me, I'm the Gingerbread Man." He galloped past a big prickly cactus and raced away as fast as his boots could carry him . . .

until he came to a herd of long-horned cattle grazing in a field. "Mmmm. No more grass for us!" they all cried. "We want gingerbread!"

But the Gingerbread Cowboy just laughed and said, "Giddyup, giddyup as fast as you can. You can't catch me, I'm the Gingerbread Man." He ducked between their legs and raced away as fast as his boots could carry him . . .

until he met some hungry cowboys riding the range. The cowboys yelled, "Stampede!" They wanted gingerbread too.

The Gingerbread Cowboy just laughed and said, "Giddyup, giddyup as fast as you can. You can't catch me, I'm the Gingerbread Man." He turned down a canyon and raced away as fast as his boots could carry him . . .

until he met a coyote napping in the sun. Now, the Gingerbread Cowboy was feeling mighty pleased with himself. "I've run from the rancher and his wife, the roadrunner, the javelinas, the long-horned cattle, and the cowboys," he bragged. "And I can run from you too."

The coyote smiled. "I don't want to chase you," he said. "But I can hear those folks coming fast, and there's a river just ahead. Hop onto my tail, and I'll take you across."

"I can't let them catch me now!" cried the Gingerbread Cowboy. So he hopped onto the coyote's tail.

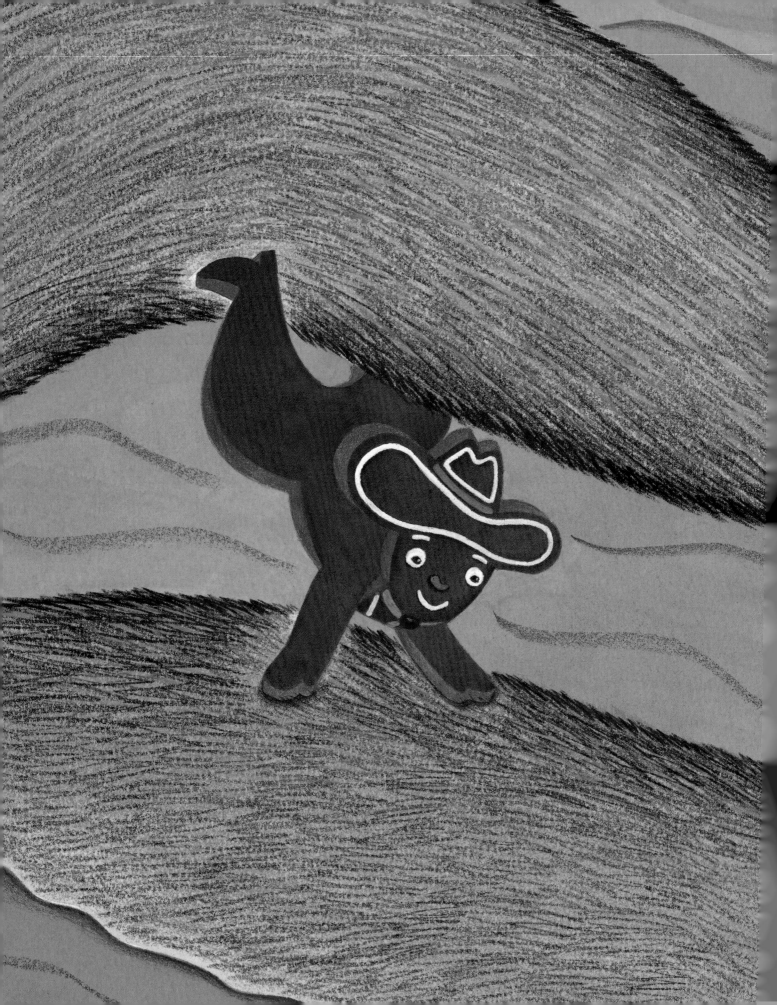

The coyote splashed into the river and began to swim. "It rained last night, and the river is deep. You'd better get on my back," said the coyote. So the Gingerbread Cowboy climbed onto the coyote's back.

By now the cowboys, the longhorns, the javelinas, the roadrunner, the rancher, and his wife had arrived at the edge of the river. The rancher's wife took out her lariat and swung a loop out toward the Gingerbread Cowboy.

"Quick! Stand on my nose!" said the coyote. So the Gingerbread Cowboy jumped up onto the coyote's nose.

"Ha! Ha! Ha!" shouted the Gingerbread Cowboy as the lasso fell short. "They missed!"

"But I won't," said the coyote.

He tossed the **G**ingerbread **C**owboy into the air like a flapjack on a griddle and swallowed him in one gulp.

And that was the end of the Gingerbread Cowboy.